Especially for baby Arthur, with love
~ M. C. B.

For my cousin Jessica Smith
~ T. M.

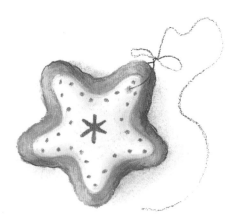

tiger tales
5 River Road, Suite 128, Wilton, CT 06897
Published in the United States 2017
Originally published in Great Britain 2017
by Little Tiger Press
Text copyright © 2017 M. Christina Butler
Illustrations copyright © 2017 Tina Macnaughton
ISBN-13: 978-1-68010-068-6
ISBN-10: 1-68010-068-8
Printed in China
LTP/1800/1819/0217
10 9 8 7 6 5 4 3 2 1

For more insight and activities, visit us at www.tigertalesbooks.com

One Cozy Christmas

by M. Christina Butler   Illustrated by Tina Macnaughton

tiger tales

It was a cold winter day, and Little Hedgehog and his friends were looking for a Christmas tree.

"This one! This one!" squeaked the baby mice.

"Perfect!" beamed Little Hedgehog. "I'm so happy you could all stay for Christmas. It's going to be wonderful!"

"Oh, Christmas tree,
Oh, Christmas tree,
How lovely are
your branches,"
the mice sang merrily
on the way home.

Everyone helped with
decorating the tree, and
soon it sparkled and shone.
"It's so beautiful," sighed
Little Hedgehog.
"Hooray for Christmastime with
friends!" they all cheered on
their way to bed.

But the next morning, everyone was in a terrible mood!

"Ouch!" cried Fox. "You stepped on my paws!"

"I can't find my socks!" moaned Rabbit.

"Never mind your socks!" grumbled Badger.

"Who was snoring all night long?"

"And who's been eating the decorations?" squeaked a baby mouse. "We hung seven cookies on the tree yesterday, and now there are only six!"

"Stop!" cried Little Hedgehog. "We shouldn't argue at Christmastime! Let's do something fun. Should we go skating?"

"Yes!" said the baby mice, and they all set off to the pond.

Sliding and gliding across the ice, the friends were soon laughing again. They twirled until they were all tired out. Then, with frosty paws, they skated home.

As he warmed up with cookies and hot chocolate, Little Hedgehog smiled to himself. *I can't wait for Christmas to come!* he thought.

"I hope you sleep well, Badger," said
Little Hedgehog as they headed to bed.
"Thank you," yawned Badger. "Let's hope
there won't be any more snoring."

But in the morning, the friends were grumpier than ever!
"That snoring was awful!" complained Badger.
"I was awake all night!" Fox snapped.
"Fox," grumbled Mouse, "you're squishing my
Christmas sweater!"
But that wasn't all . . . .

"Someone's eaten another cookie!" called
a baby mouse.

"Wait! Something even more terrible has
happened!" cried Little Hedgehog. "I can't
find my HAT!"

"This is terrible!" cried Rabbit. "We must find Little Hedgehog's hat!"

But even though they searched high and low all morning . . .

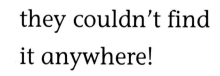

they couldn't find it anywhere!

Little Hedgehog watched sadly as the mice played in the snow. It was too cold to go outside without his hat.

"I can't even go into my own kitchen," he sniffed, "because Fox is baking a surprise. This isn't how things are supposed to be at all!"

At dinnertime, as he dug into Fox's delicious cake, Little Hedgehog began to feel a little better. The tree twinkled in the glow of the fire, and Badger read exciting stories to them.

"It's almost Christmas!" giggled the baby mice excitedly, clapping their paws.
But poor Little Hedgehog was still thinking about his hat. "It's such a mystery!" he mumbled.

That night, Little Hedgehog hardly slept a wink.
The house echoed with giggles, squeaks, and
a strange click-clicking sound.

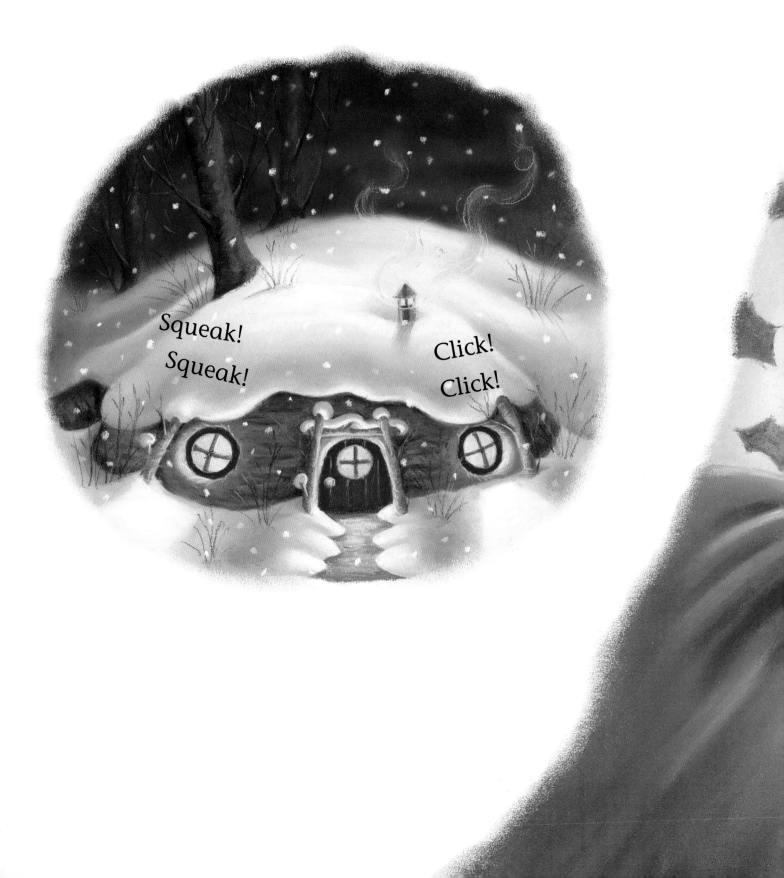

But when the first rays of the morning
sun streamed in through the window,
Little Hedgehog leapt out of bed.
"It's Christmas morning!" he cried happily,
completely forgetting how sleepy he was.

"Merry Christmas, everyone!" sang Little Hedgehog as the friends gathered to open their presents.

"We stayed up to paint you this picture!" squeaked the baby mice.

"And this is from me!" smiled Badger.

"What a nice new hat, Badger!" cried Little Hedgehog. "That click-clicking noise last night must have been your knitting needles!"

Everyone was merrily
unwrapping their gifts
when all of a sudden
Mouse cried, "Oh my
goodness! The Christmas
tree is snoring!"

"What could it be?" cried Little Hedgehog.
And when he looked, he couldn't believe his eyes!
"Oh!" he cried. "I've found my hat . . . and there's
someone asleep inside it!"

The friends looked down at a little squirrel, fast asleep.

"He must have been asleep in the tree when we brought it home," whispered Badger.

"That explains the snoring!" added Fox. "And the missing cookies!"

"Well, I'm glad my old hat found a good home," smiled Little Hedgehog. "How wonderful to share Christmas with my dear friends . . . and a brand-new one, too!"

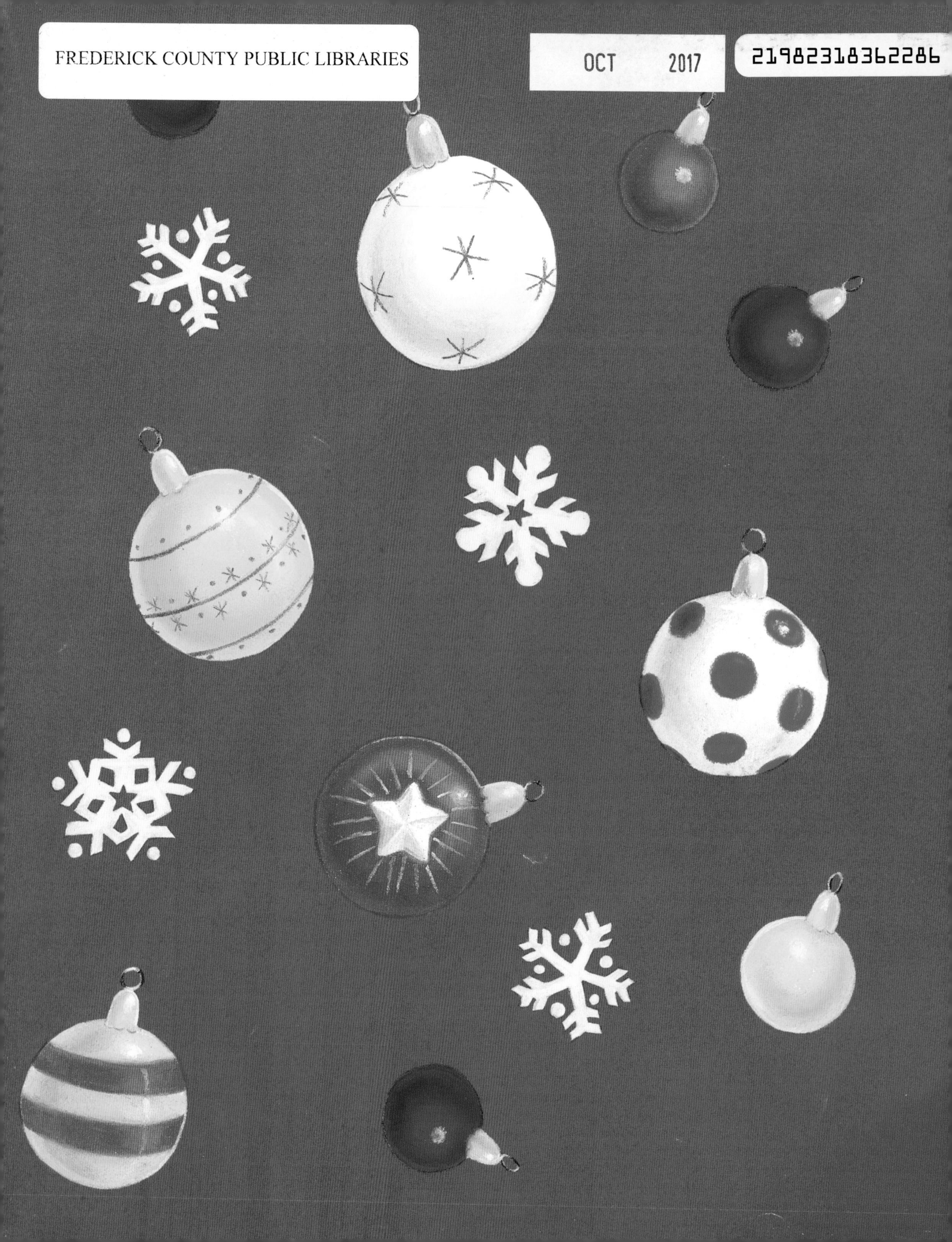